HARRY HUGGER AND THE PLAYFUL PUPPY

What happens when Harry finds someone
who gives more hugs than him?

Dedication

"Everyone thinks they have the best dog.
And none of them are wrong."

– W.R. Purche

Inspired by

Taylor, Grayson, Paula and Lily

Editors

Madi Foley and Mark Ramsay

Associate Editors

Annabelle, Simon, Harrison and Veronica

Maxton, Corbin and Logan

Harry had been awake most of the night. He was so excited. Today was the day they were going to get a furry friend.

As the sun rose, so did Harry. He quickly followed his morning routine. He brushed his teeth, combed his hair, and ate a buttery, brown bagel.

Harry picked out a colorful bow tie. This bow tie matched the new, small bow tie they had previously purchased.

Harry remembered back to last week and the moment when his tiny merry Mom and his big daring Dad said they could adopt a playful puppy.

Harry and Harriet had spent every spare moment since on the computer, looking at the rescue shelter website. The website had descriptions and photos of lots of dogs. The dogs were of all ages, colors, shapes and sizes. All of them looked like they just wanted a happy home.

His parents were now awake. Harriet was also up, dressed and bouncing on her tiny toes. Using his hugging superpower, Harry hugged Harriet, his tiny merry Mom and his big daring Dad.

Daring Dad and merry Mom reminded Harry and Harriet
of the promises they had made. They had promised to feed,
water and clean up after the puppy, every day, without being
told. They would be in charge of giving the puppy baths, and
the puppy would have to sleep in its own little bouncy bed.

It was time to go. Harry and his family hopped in their red ride.

They arrived at the pet shelter. They had called ahead to let them know they were coming. The Huggers could hear what sounded like a hundred happy hounds.

Linda, the lovely shelter lady, asked them some questions.
How big? How old? Did they want a "sleepy snuggler," a "crazy
clown" or a "rapid racer?"

Once they had described their ideal dog, Linda asked wonderful Wayne to help them find their perfect puppy playmate. Harry asked Wayne if they could meet a puppy Harry had seen on the worldwide website.

Wayne brought that puppy and took them to a special area, away from the noise and distractions of the other dogs. The puppy looked just like his photo. The puppy did not seem interested in the happy Huggers.

Harry and Harriet were sad. They thought the puppy was the one for them. Wayne told them they would know when they had met the dog that was their perfect furry fit.

They met a few more dogs, but none seemed to be the right furry fit. Harry was beginning to wonder if they would ever find their puppy. Through the fence, the Huggers could see Linda and Wayne excitedly talking. There was a dog that was not exactly what the Huggers had described, but Linda trusted her shelter, matchmaking, super senses.

Wayne brought the puppy in to meet the Huggers. There was a long awkward moment as the dog stood near Wayne and looked droopily down.

The puppy slowly looked up and saw Harry. Suddenly, the puppy took two big steps and leapt into Harry's arms. As Harry hugged the puppy, the puppy hugged Harry and buried its nose into Harry's chest. Somehow the dog knew that Harry was a huge hugger.

Everyone knew this puppy was their forever furry fit. Wayne encouraged them to take the puppy on a walk around the shelter just to be sure. With every step, the puppy looked up to see what they wanted him to do. The Huggers agreed they should adopt this hugging, playful puppy.

Harry's Mom and Dad filled out the paperwork, paid the fees and promised to send photos of the puppy to the shelter. Before they got into the car, Harry stopped and pulled out the small bow tie that matched his own. He placed it on the playful puppy. The puppy seemed to know this was his forever family.

They arrived home and introduced the playful puppy to his new home. He sniffed everything, ran around and excitedly explored.

Harry and Harriet had the huge responsibility of choosing a name for the playful puppy. They wrote down a short list of possible names: Harper, Henry, Hudson, Hayden, Harrison, Holden, Hayes, Hector, Huxley, Hezekiah, Holland, Hadlee, Harlan, Houston, Henrik, Hassan, Harold, Hugh, Howard, Hugo, Harvey, Hank.

Then it occurred to Harry and Harriet. They would let the reader of this book name the playful puppy. Here is a place for you to write the playful puppy's new name.

_____

There is a lot you must do for a new, playful puppy on his first day in his forever home. Daring Dad taught everyone how to take the playful puppy out for potty breaks. Harry and Harriet split up their work. Harry set out the food and water bowls. Harriet readied the dog's bouncy bed.

They loved that, when anyone sat down, the playful puppy would jump into their arms and give them a huge hug. The playful puppy was indeed a furry fit.

There is a lot you must do for a new, playful puppy on his first day in his forever home. Daring Dad taught everyone how to take the playful puppy out for potty breaks. Harry and Harriet split up their work. Harry set out the food and water bowls. Harriet readied the dog's bouncy bed.

They loved that, when anyone sat down, the playful puppy would jump into their arms and give them a huge hug. The playful puppy was indeed a furry fit.

As bedtime approached, the playful puppy, Harry and Harriet were getting sleepy. The playful puppy watched as Harry got ready for bed. The puppy stayed by his side as he brushed his teeth and washed his friendly face.

As they always do, Harry and his family had a great group hug. Harry, Harriet, Mom, Dad and the playful puppy wrapped their arms around each other and squeezed tightly. Harry thought to take a memory picture, in his head, so he would not forget this magical moment.

As bedtime approached, the playful puppy, Harry and Harriet were getting sleepy. The playful puppy watched as Harry got ready for bed. The puppy stayed by his side as he brushed his teeth and washed his friendly face.

As they always do, Harry and his family had a great group hug. Harry, Harriet, Mom, Dad and the playful puppy wrapped their arms around each other and squeezed tightly. Harry thought to take a memory picture, in his head, so he would not forget this magical moment.

Merry Mom put the playful puppy in his new bouncy bed. Lying in his bed, Harry smiled. He had found someone who also had his hugging superpower. Today would be the first of many days of awesome adventures. Within moments, Harry was delightfully dozing.

Harry was awakened by a noise. It was late at night; the noise was sad, and it was coming from the side of his bed. Harry looked down and saw the playful puppy. Harry thought, He is super scared and likely lonely.

Harry thought maybe, just this once, it would be OK if the playful puppy slept in his big bed. The playful puppy jumped into Harry's bed and snuggled in for a huge hug. As Harry was falling asleep, the playful puppy gave him a loving lick.

---The Beginning---